P9-ASG-484

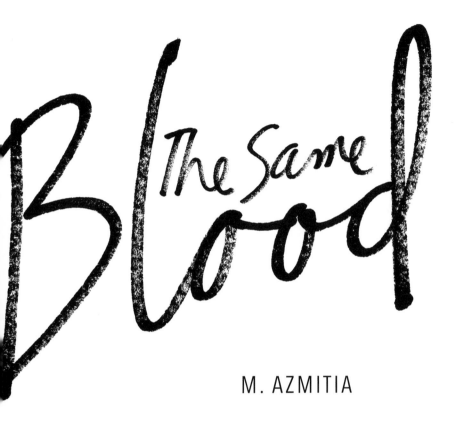

The Same Blood

M. AZMITIA

An imprint of Enslow Publishing

WEST **44** BOOKS™

Please visit our website, www.west44books.com.
For a free color catalog of all our high-quality books,
call toll free 1-800-542-2595 or fax 1-877-542-2596.

Cataloging-in-Publication Data

Names: Azmitia, M.
Title: The same blood / M. Azmitia.
Description: New York : West 44, 2019. | Series: West 44 YA verse
Identifiers: ISBN 9781538382516 (pbk.) | ISBN 9781538382523
  (library bound) | ISBN 9781538383261 (ebook)
Subjects: LCSH: Children's poetry, American. | Children's poetry,
  English. | English poetry.
Classification: LCC PS586.3 S264 2019 | DDC 811'.60809282--dc23

First Edition

Published in 2019 by
Enslow Publishing LLC
101 West 23rd Street, Suite #240
New York, NY 10011

Editor: Caitie McAneney
Designer: Seth Hughes

Printed in the United States of America

CPSIA compliance information: Batch #CS18W44: For further information contact
Enslow Publishing LLC, New York, New York at 1-800-542-2595.

To everyone I ever loved

You have foggy memories
of Puerto Rico. Hazy.

Like a dream you can
never quite grasp come
morning.

You remember
being six years old. Stepping

barefoot

into an orange-
tiled fountain
with Mel.

　　　　Finding your shoes in
　　　　grass overrun with ants.

You remember
a beach,

deserted

and covered in
seaweed.

Green waves
that knocked you back
onto the shore.

Mel laughing as
she helped you
stand—
    You okay, Elena?

        The way you sulked
        because it wasn't safe
        for you to swim.

When a volcano's
ash keeps you from

        flying home,

you cry and tell Mami
you miss your dog.

Mel tells it differently.

She writes poetry about it
for the next 10 years.

She gets that

faraway

look in her eyes
when she talks about it.

Like
if she looks hard
enough, maybe

just maybe

she can still see
the island.

Sometimes

you think that Mel
remembers
a different Puerto Rico.

One with a sweet-
smelling breeze.

With the soothing chirp
of coquis
in the dark.

With wild horses
eating free-
growing coffee beans
in the mountains.

Mel cries when
she finds blue tiles
hidden among the grass

in the place where
Mami's childhood home
once stood.

She begs Papi for just
a few days more.

She keeps begging
as you climb
into a stuffy taxi.

She keeps begging
as you make your
way to the airport.

From that day forward
she doesn't let
anyone but you
call her Mel.

She insists on
introducing herself as

Marianella

and rolling her *R's*
as though her tongue
is native.

At the time you roll
your eyes.

But
after you lose her,
you think maybe

there were parts
of her that
she never shared
with you.

Parts of her
that may have been

left on the island.

You and Mel
shared a face

and almost
nothing else.

There was a
softness to her that
you never had—

   as though her
   extra three minutes in

   the womb
   stripped her

of the sharp
edges you
always had.

At five years old, you and Mel
strung cardboard boxes
together with yarn.

Drew wheels on the sides.
Put a hat on a bean-filled bear
and called him a conductor.

Filled the other boxes
with toys and dragged the
"train" around the
apartment.

You made up stops—

Candyland, for some.
The moon, for others.

One by one until
the train was empty

and you'd swept the whole
house with your clothes.

At nine, the map went up
in Mel's room.

She took down posters
of her favorite bands
to make space.

The whole world laid out
for the two of you.

One day you'd see
the world together.

In a boat?
you suggested.

        In a houseboat!
        she'd agreed.

You found tacks in
the kitchen—red for
Mel, blue for you.

You marked all
the places you'd visit.

Each one was a plan—

a promise.

By 11, you started
to think Mel wasn't
running to those places
with you.

The nervous feelings
came to her more often.

She told you she had
dreams of another
life.

One where she wasn't
afraid, not weighted
down by—

> *this*,
> she'd said,
> pointing to her chest.

◊

Back then,

you could distract
her with a joke, a
marathon of her
favorite shows.

It stopped being so simple
not long after.

Later,
you'll realize

Mel was never running
away with you.

She was running
away from herself.

Before you moved
into the bigger house,

back when you
shared a room:

you could hear her
some nights.

Crying quietly as
you drifted off
          into
                    sleep.

Always for reasons
she couldn't explain

when you asked her
about it over breakfast
the next morning.

Other times

she'd twist her
hands until welts

rose up on her
skin.

She'd beg Mami
and Papi

to let her stay home
from school.

Because of the sudden,
unexplained feeling

of pure *dread*.

Like something horrible
was waiting for her

outside the door.

Papi had no patience
for her.

Would keep
pressing her for

       answers
       that she never had.

He'd give you
that tired look

as if to ask why
she couldn't be tough,

like you.

Mami held Mel's
hand and kissed her
curls.

Told her to pray.

But you could always see:

the way Mami's
comforting words rolled
off of Mel and never
quieted her mind—

you may have been

the only one

who could *see.*

You don't want
a *quinceañera.*

You beg for money
instead for
a trip to London.

But Mel insists.
Es importante, she
tells you after
your parents have
gone to sleep.

She paints your nails
and you answer her
in English. Tell her

she can have
her own *quince,* but

even as you say the words
you know the answer.

A birthday party
for just one twin

is silly at best,
cruel at worst.

So one week later,
there you sit.

Checking the time
and texting your friends

as she tries on another
oversized red ball gown.

When you're not watching,
she looks to you
for approval.

You don't see the way
her
    face
        falls

as she realizes
how much you don't care.

The party is a joke
and you know it.

The white friends
you invited
know it too.

You smile for
the cameras but
roll your eyes

when your family's
back is turned.

You don't try to hide
how awkward you feel

in the spotlight

as your mother slips
the shiny new high heels
onto your feet

while the crowd
watches from
the dark.

Marianella cries

as Papi does
the same for her,

hugs him tight
before walking out
onto the dance floor

with him.

As soon as
the toasts are done

your heels are
in your hand.

And you're having
a smoke

with your friends
behind the building.

They all laugh

at how dramatic
the party's rituals are.

And you don't
        agree

but you don't really
        disagree
        either.

Months from now,

when Mel is gone,

you'll wonder if this
was the moment

you began to lose her.

The only night
you dared to ask Mel
if she was
            okay,

she didn't answer.

            Instead,
she walked right past
you,

            on her way to
the kitchen. Clutching

a blanket around
her shoulders.

            As if she
was afraid of what
her hands might do

if she let go.

Later that night,

you saw Mami
in Mel's room

through the cracked
open door.

She was muttering
prayers under her
breath

as she held Mel
close:

You need to pray, mija.

*Ask God to take
these feelings away.*

And a single
white
candle

flickered on Mel's dresser.

By the time Mami
went back to her own
room,

> the candle
> hadn't stopped burning

> and Mel
> hadn't stopped crying.

She stared blankly
at the flame
but didn't
seem to
> *see* it.

She didn't see you,
standing

in her doorway, searching

for the right words
and coming up

empty.

Here's a lie you tell yourself:

that you never knew
anything was wrong.

That once you
and Mel
had your own rooms,

you never heard the
crying again.

That you didn't know
she tried to drown it out
with loud music

but never quite
succeeded
in muffling her sobs.

That you never
raised your hand
          to knock.

Never stopped
when you realized

you didn't know
what to *say.*

That there was
nothing you could do

about the panic attacks
when she begged you

not to tell Mami
and Papi.

That you didn't
cover for her when

her guidance counselor
asked too
          many
                    questions.

That you were so *sure*
she was kidding

all those times
she joked about
being

dead.

That you never thought
there was a chance
she might
take
        it
                too
                        far.

That when you come home
from soccer practice
after school that day,

there's not some part
of you that isn't
surprised

to find your sister,

        barely breathing,

on her bedroom floor.

They all ask you—

Mami,
      Papi,
             your friends,
                         the therapist

                         they make you see
                         after Mel is gone—

and every time
you say you didn't know.

That you had no idea
anything was wrong,

even though all
you can think about
is how it was impossible

not to know.

When you were small,

Papi
had a bottle
for every occasion.

Rum was for good days:
        for birthdays
        and anniversaries
        and his promotion
        to Sergeant.

Whiskey was for bad days:
        for when his hands
        shook

        as he set down
        his shield

        and peeled off
        his uniform.

For when only
a tumbler full of

amber

could steady him.

But that was
before.

The first night you

and Mami

and Papi

come home without
        Mel,

you can see
that quiver
in Papi's hands.

Searching
for something to ground
him in this new
life.

But the bottles
are gone, and you
wonder

which one
he would have reached for

in moments of mourning.

The shrine goes up
on the very
          next
                    day.

Mami tells you
not to call it that.

Tells you that it's an altar.
But as far as you know,

Mel was not a god.
Is not a god.

And that's her picture
up there.

The shrine starts with an
8x11-inch photo

of Mel at the *quinceañera*—
just six months ago—

but it grows quickly
as if it's alive.

Family members come
from
        far away

to add
their own flowers
to the table.

To light a candle
in Mel's name.

The smell of
sulfur-burning matches
sticks to the couch.

The photo blurs
in the heat
of all the flames.

Your stomach
        turns
each time you walk past.

It's dark
except where her face
is lit up in a tribute
        you had no part in.

You see her face
in the shadows.

Your heart stops
when you think,

        for just a moment,

she might still be here.

There are people
in your living room
who you barely recognize.

Some of them are
sort of familiar, faces
that you can *maybe*
recall from years ago.

Others are total strangers.

Mami introduces them
        as aunts
        and uncles
        and cousins

she hasn't seen since
before you and
Mel were born.

They never met Mel,
        and yet

here they are.

Gathering around her shrine
and taking out their rosaries.

In Puerto Rico,
Mami says,

we pray rosaries
for nine days after
a death.

In Puerto Rico,
she says,

we wear bright colors
to help the spirit
rise.

In Puerto Rico,
she says,

we don't play music
for nine days,
out of respect.

But you're not
in Puerto Rico.

You're here, and Mel

is nowhere.

The fridge is stacked

full of containers with
more food than your

shrinking family

will ever need.

People keep bringing it here,
as if grief has made

you
and Mami
and Papi

forget how to use a stove.

As if you might

break

if you even try.

There's a knock
on the door

that you somehow
hear over the rosaries
being prayed in the
living room.

It's Sarah,

who is blonde
and pale
and lives next door.

She's dressed all in black
and looks like the
opposite of you,
with your dark hair
and brown skin
and mint green dress.

She's come to pay
respects to your family.

She looks past you,
into the living room.

She sees the crowd of

middle-aged
Hispanic women
in blinding
        bright
                colors

wailing
        Ave Maria
in front of a shrine
to your sister.

You take her outside
to talk where it's quiet.

There's something
in the way her shoulders
        sag
in relief.

Something in her
awkward laugh.

And the stilted way
she says,
        That was intense.

Something in the way
she looks to you

for an explanation,
or maybe a dismissal.

Somewhere in between,
you feel that drop
in your stomach,

        heavy
        and hot.
        That shame.

You wave your hand,

tell her it's just some
weird thing
your family does,

that you're not a part of it.

She laughs for real
and relaxes.

The shame in your gut
        goes sour
        and turns to guilt.

Mel's disappointment lingers
somewhere on the
back of your neck.

You can't escape it—
        you dig
        deeper
        into it.

The next time you
clean your room,

you find a long strand
of dark hair
coiled
into a tight curl.

Your hair looks like that
before you attack it
        with heat
        and brushes
        and creams
to make it go pin straight.

Mel never bothered—
she let her curls go free.

Let them be big.

Did nothing to
hide
the way you do,

did nothing to
try to blend in
the way you do.

Mel's feelings were clear:

she was a Puerto Rican girl.

You're just a girl
who happens to
be Puerto Rican.

It doesn't mean as much
to you
as it did to her.

Isn't such a vital part
of who you are.

Every time she
> brought a lunch
> to school

> that made your
> white classmates
> wrinkle their noses.

Every time
> Spanish rolled fluid
> off her tongue
> where it stumbled
> off of yours.

Every time
> she scolded someone
> for a joke they made
> at the expense
> of Latin people.

You could feel
the rift between
the two of you

grow w i d e r.

You should have been
where she was,

living without shame.

Instead
you stood on the
sidelines of your culture

and let Mel stand out all alone.

Mami checks on you.

She knocks often on
your bedroom door
when it's closed.

She paces the hall
when it's open.

She texts you
over the course
of the school day,

calls you when
you don't text back.

Some days
you sneak into
the bathroom
        to answer her calls
        in hushed tones.

To hear the panic
melt from her voice.

To assure her
that you're safe.

When Mami asks
if you're
     okay,

you know it doesn't
mean the same thing

as it did before.

There's something desperate
behind it now,
     a need
     to fix
     a mistake.

Papi does it differently.

He won't ask you outright
if you're okay,

if you ever feel like
you might want to
die.

Instead
he watches you
        like a case he's
        trying to solve.

        Like you're a suspect
        he's staking out.

        Like he's looking
        for a pattern
        or some kind of clue.

You can't help but think,
        bitterly,

that he never believed Mel

when she said
        something
        was
        wrong.

This is how Mami mourns:

She lights candles.

Thick ones in glass jars,
painted with saints.

Small oiled ones
offered to secret gods.

Rocks decorated with shells.

A woman who visits
to "cleanse" your house
with smoke.

Still,
Mami looks older
every day,

with gray hair that
wasn't there just
weeks ago.

This is how Papi mourns:

he stops talking,
barely looks up from
his plate at dinner.

With no bottles
to reach for,

he works instead.
Stays gone for 18
hours at a time,

some days.

You'd say he
looks tired

except

he doesn't seem
to feel much of
anything
        anymore.

In those
rare moments

when you see Mami and
Papi in a room
together,

they're like

flint
        and steel.

Each time they
talk, some part
of them burns away

with each shouted word.

As they try to cast blame
on each other but shoulder it

alone

all the same.

This is how you mourn:

You don't.

Nothing is wrong.

You don't reach for Mel
in your sleep.

You don't look into
her room
to see what she's doing.

You don't wait for
her after school before
walking home alone.

You don't grit
your teeth to push
down the guilt

that threatens to
shatter you

from the inside.

As a family,

you choose your words
carefully,

as if the wrong
ones might disturb
the air around you.

As if the ground
might splinter
and swallow you whole.

As if saying
Mel's name would
rip
      you
           open

and bare your pain
for the world to see.

It takes some adjusting.

Papi cooks too
much, makes enough
rice for four

and sets an extra place
at the table.

Mami calls you
by the wrong name
sometimes,

then touches your
hair as if to remind
herself.

And absolutely

no one

can bear to look
at your face anymore.

Mami says therapy will help.

Not just you,
she says,
but everyone.

You tell her there's
no point.

That there's nothing
to talk about.

> That Mel was the one
> who needed therapy.

That sitting on a couch
and telling a stranger

> that your sister is dead

won't bring her back.

Mami looks at you
as though she doesn't
know who you are,

and Papi says nothing at all.

Your therapist's name
          is Tiana.

Mami goes first,
tells her that your
family is "struggling."

You roll your eyes.

You tell Tiana
that you're not
                    crazy.
(Not like Mel was.)

That Mami is
overreacting.

That you're not sure
why you're here.

Papi is silent

as usual.

You don't tell her

that you've never had
to exist alone
and now
you don't know how.

You don't tell her

that you know exactly
who to blame.

You don't tell her

that your indifference
killed your sister.

You keep the words
locked behind your tongue

as if releasing them

would make them real.

♦

You're in the hall at school
when it hits you:

that feeling of freedom,

of being truly on
your own.

Of not having Mel,
like an angel on your
shoulder,

forcing you to do
the right thing.

Telling you not to skip class.

Trying to guilt you
into joining school clubs
so she doesn't have to
do it alone.

Making you worry about her
even when she's not there.

Suddenly
you're only responsible
for one person,

and you breathe
as if for the first time.

And you push down
the voice
in the back of your mind.

The one
that warns you of
        trouble
        ahead.

You quit soccer
the next day.

      And Yearbook Club.

            And going to classes
            you don't
            care about.

You sneak out
behind the building
and smoke a cigarette.

Let go of the
ball of nerves in
your gut

telling you to go
back inside.

For the first time

there is no one there

to tell you otherwise.

Suddenly
there's all this time.

> Time to sit at home
> and watch the shows
> Mel hated.

> Time to hang out
> with the friends at
> school

> that Mel never
> got along with.

> Time to be
> Elena

> without being
> *Elena and Marianella.*

So why
isn't that enough

to calm the guilt

that twists
        and burns

just under your skin?

You get a text
one weekend

from a girl at
school
called Angie.

Once, in eighth grade,
she asked,

*Why don't you
celebrate
Cinco de Mayo?*

                              *We're Puerto
                              Rican, not
                              Mexican,*
                              Mel told her.

What's the difference?
Angie asked,
laughing.

                              Mel never liked her.

Angie is inviting you
to a party.

Your fingers begin
to type out an excuse:

> *sorry busy*
>
> *thanks, not*
> *feeling good*
>
> *maybe next time*

But Mel
is not here
to tell you no.

You accept.

> *when and where?*

◖

Mami watches you
get ready that night.

Helps you straighten
the curled strands of
hair near
your forehead.

Lends you her
favorite pair of
boots.

Asks if you
need perfume.

> *El señor te bendiga,*
> she says,
> just before you
> leave.

Though you didn't
ask her
for a blessing.

You think she
might be close to
tears.

So you shut the
door behind you

and don't look back.

For a moment

you think you
could actually forget.

In between the
clumps of people
milling

      around the kitchen.

      In the living-room-
      turned-dance-floor.

      The couples
      whispering together
      in the hall—

you think you
might be moving on.

You wonder
if this is what

life
          beyond
                    grief

looks like.

But then
you're in the kitchen,

grabbing an extra
soda for Mel.

And you flush
as you realize

it won't be that easy.

It starts with one.

Angie's friends arrive.

They're older than her
and armed with
familiar-looking
bottles of amber.

She offers to mix
something for you.

She pulls the soda
out of your hand

She pours it into
a plastic red cup

along with whatever
is in those bottles.

The smell reminds you
of Papi,

years ago,
before—

before he—

You almost don't
take the cup—

remember all the warnings
Papi gave you,

the horror stories of
how he almost lost

> his job
> and Mami
> and you
> and Mel.

But you also remember
the way one sip could

> turn his sorrows
> into something softer.

> Still his shaking hands.

> Quiet his mind
> for just a moment.

You take the cup.

◖

Something in you
unties itself.

Loosens the jumble
of your thoughts
with each swallow.

The tips of your
fingers and toes
    tingle

in a way they never
did after the beers
you've had
here and there,

in another life.

You relax your shoulders
for the first time
in months.

Laugh
like you forgot
you could.

You don't just
forget

that Mel is gone,

that your parents
aren't coping,

that *you*
aren't coping.

For a little while
you forget

that you had
a sister at all.

And you can't
bring yourself

to feel bad.

You have another

and another

and another.

Some part of you hopes
that with enough,

this feeling
will never
go away.

But then it's late,
and Papi is calling.

Asking how long
you'll be, if you
need a ride home.

You choose your
words carefully.

Talk slow and steady.

Tell him Angie
will drive you.

Later that night

after Angie
forces you to
drink some water.

After she carefully
drives you home.

After you've tip-
toed upstairs
and crawled into bed.

You wait for Papi
to realize what you've
done,

but he doesn't.

Even the next morning,

when he asks you
how it went as
he gets ready for work,

he doesn't see.

Relief washes over
you,

and you smile.

You do it again
the next weekend.

And the weekend after that.

Sometimes
you go to Angie's
on a school night,

when her parents
aren't home.

And you do it then, too.

Soon all you do
is forget.

Forget about school.

About Mel.

About Mami
and Papi.

About the shrine
still in your
living room.

About the sour
feelings that
keep you up
at night.

Soon, all there is

is the haze of it
all passing by.

And the freedom
of forgetting.

You overdo it one night.

You forget
that you have therapy
the next morning.

Wear sunglasses
to Tiana's office.

You don't need to be here—

                you've found the cure
                for all your blues.

You let Mami and Papi
do the talking.

(Mostly Mami.)

And you wait
for the world to
darken.

◊

Tiana notices—

says she'd like to
see you for
a few sessions
alone.

You'd roll your
eyes if it wouldn't
make your head
throb.

Before you can say
no, Mami is making
an appointment.

You can feel control
slipping out of
your hands.

The thing about
letting go of guilt

is that you never
really knew

how much there was.

       Before Sarah.

       Before Mel was gone.

       Even before the
       quinceañera.

There it was:
the feeling

that you were an
imposter
in a Latina's skin.

That you weren't
Puerto Rican enough.

Because you couldn't
speak Spanish.

Because you didn't
like all of the food
on the island.

Because sometimes,
being Latina
was *tiring*.

And you just wanted to
blend in.

That bottle touches
your lips,

and years of shame
melt away.

♦

Things you can do
without Mel:

- Delete her *novelas*
  from the DVR.

- Be lazy.

- Stop worrying about
  your future or
  the state of the world.

- Go to parties without
  being dragged home
  because she was
  getting anxious.

- Drink without that
  worried look—
  without that frantic
  whisper of
        But you remember
        what happened to Papi…

- Kiss a soft-haired, green-
  eyed white boy from
  school without
  wondering if he thinks
  you're *exotic*.

After a while,

you get good at it.

You don't even flinch
anymore when you
down a shot.

You don't hesitate
to try whatever is
in the cup
Angie passes to you.

Most nights
you don't even get
sick anymore.

You don't end the night
hunched over a toilet

or a trash can

or the sewer drain
on the sidewalk.

♦

You get even better
at hiding.

You pack a few extra
things in your bag before
you leave.

Make sure to brush
your teeth before
you go home. Cover
the smell of alcohol
with perfume.

Sometimes
you come home and
have whole

conversations
with Mami
or Papi

without them noticing.

You've learned to
keep your words

steady

no matter how
unsteady
your mind is.

Learned how to make
your arms and legs work
when they don't
want to.

You keep waiting
for them to notice—

you almost *want* them
to notice—

but they don't.

Part of you wants to
s c r e a m.

To ask if they learned
nothing
from failing Mel.

But you drown that part out

with another shot.

Spring passes
in a blur of plastic
red cups.

In pointless
therapy sessions.

In the lies you feed
your teachers

when they ask
why you've stopped
trying.

Still

you pass every class and
can't help but see
pity
behind every
decent grade.

You're not sure why
your teachers/
guidance counselors/
every adult you know

would pity you.

Your friends don't.

Not when you're sitting on
your new friend's bedroom
floor,

passing a joint to the
next person.

Not when you're wasted in
the backseat of Angie's
car,

laughing
and *living*

as she swerves a
little to the right.

You're not the girl
with the dead sister.
Not to them.

You're just *Elena.*

The girl who laughs at
everyone's dumb
jokes

and can throw back a
shot without
flinching.

Why would they pity you
when you're living
the life

you always imagined was
just beyond your grasp,

with no one there
to stop you?

Tiana doesn't ask
about Mel.

Instead she asks

> about school,

> about your friends,

> about Mami and
> Papi.

> Never about Mel.

You start to get
creative

with the lies you
tell her:

> You win awards
> at school.

> Do volunteer work
> with your friends.

> Settle fights between
> Mami and Papi.

You don't think she
believes you, but
she never calls your bluff.

You wonder what
magical answer you can
give her

to get out of this.

To make her believe

that you're okay.

Spring melts
into summer.

Into counting down
the days until
vacation.

And into bright, hot
sun that tans your
brown skin browner
with every minute spent
outside.

Angie invites you over
on that last day of
school.

It turns out to be a
going-away party.

She's leaving for Spain
for the whole summer
in the morning.

She speaks near-
perfect Spanish, you
discover.

You drown out the
shame that fact brings
with another beer.

You float around the
party, talk to your other
friends.

They all have plans:

> Chris follows Angie
> to Spain in a week.

> Eddie's got a summer
> job.

> *Space camp,* Janey says,
> bouncing
> and giddy.

Road trips

and internships

and family
vacations

all around.

And then there's you:

> no plan,
> no future.

> Sitting on your
> hands in this
> dumpy town.

Suddenly
there's all this quiet.

No friends to fill
the space or silence.

No school to pretend
you care about.

Mami spends more
and more
time away from home.

She invites you to
join her for a

"cleansing"

but you shake your
head and go back
to bed.

Papi is still out there trying
to save the world.

While you sit at
home, wondering if
it was always this
quiet.

Or if Mel kept you
from noticing.

Mel.

You haven't thought
about her—

really thought
about her—

in weeks.

Around this time
of year, she'd be
dragging you to
the beach, where

you'd think of
fun birthday plans.

Every year she'd ask,
with some hope in
her voice, if you wanted
to go back to
Puerto Rico.

And every year you'd
ignore the way her face
fell
when you said,
        Not really.

You try to pass
the time

by studying for your
driver's test.

But it's hard to
focus in this quiet,

when some part of
you keeps listening for
the sound of footsteps
upstairs.

For music coming
from Mel's room.

It's hard to forget
about her here, without
friends

or drinks

or lies

to distract you.

Here it's just you

and the ghost of Mel

that seems to linger
in every room.

You watch TV to avoid it.

You eat to avoid it.

You sleep to avoid it.

But every time
there's something that won't
let you forget.

> A joke that Mel
> would have loved.

> A meal that Mel
> would have made better.

> A memory of Mel's face
> when you found her on
> the floor that day.

And with it all
comes the same thought

you've been desperate
to escape.

The one that tells you
there's blood on your hands.

That you're to blame.

Just as much
as if you'd forced Papi's
sleeping pills

into her mouth
yourself.

Where is this coming from?

You were over this

you were fine

you were moving on

you were *living*

how is this happening

why is this happening

it was all your f a u l t

     your fault

         your fault

            your—

◊

For the first time
in your life,

you wake up on
a birthday that is
yours

and yours alone.

As you wake, your
first thought

is that *quinceañera*,
the last birthday you'd
ever share with
Mel.

You think of those sparkling
heels, sitting in a
dusty box in your
closet.

You think of how you
would've been better
to her if you'd known.

Mami and Papi take
you to dinner.

They let you pick the
place, as if that makes
this a normal day.

Mami's eyes are still
swollen after all the
crying she did

when she thought
you couldn't hear.

But now, sitting across
from you with Papi,
there's a strength to her

that you haven't seen in months—
some resolve you wish
you had.

◈

It's there in Papi, too.

You feel like he's *here*,
present
in a way you've missed.

They're getting better—

working, still,
but better.

Better, like you thought
you were.

You push the roasted
carrots around on
your plate.

You wanted a Sweet Sixteen,
once. Now, more than
anything, you just want

to disappear.

You need to get out.

In the car on the way
home, you text everyone
you can think of—

friends
and sort-of friends
and near strangers—

desperate for a distraction.

It works.

You don't even change
out of your nice
dinner clothes

before you're out the door.

You go to someone's
house,

a friend of a
        friend of a
                friend of a
                        stranger.

Someone you may
have met in passing
once, weeks ago.

It doesn't matter.

All that matters
is that someone you
sort of know

is pouring you a drink.

You keep going
until the night begins to
blur past you.

People you kind-of know
herd you in different
directions.

Through the kitchen.

Into the living room.

Onto some boy who
dances pressed against
your back.

He tries to take your
hand and pull you
upstairs.

But a nice-looking
girl says she needs you
outside instead.

Careful with him,
she whispers once you're
standing in the yard.

She passes you a joint a
few minutes later.

You take it without
thinking much of it.

Suddenly
she's pulling you by
the hand onto the
sidewalk.

Suddenly
someone is dropping
a set of car keys into
your palm.

> *I'm too messed up
> to drive,* she says.

Suddenly
you're behind the
wheel of a car you've
never seen before.

Someone in the
backseat is telling you
to drive to a store you
don't know.

You start the car and
put your hands on
the wheel anyway.

You just barely got
your learner's permit.

You try to focus on one
thing at a time:

    Your foot on the gas.

        Your foot on the brake.

            The curve of the road.

        The signs you can just
        see under streetlights.

    The sound of laughter
    from the backseat.

        The click of a lighter.

            The smell of weed
            drifting through the car.

You shake your head,
close your eyes for
a second too long.

The guy in the front
seat next to you—
          what was his name?—
tells you to stop
swerving so much.

          The red and blue
          lights in the rearview.

                    The sharp *whoop*
                    of a siren.

License and registration,
the officer says.

Where's your ID?
Whose car is this?

How old are you, miss?

It's your birthday,
it's Mel's—

Have you been drinking?

Why won't your mouth
work right, just—

*Is there marijuana
in the car?*

Is there—who—

Step out of the car.

More cops.

Handcuffs tightened
on your wrists.

Your new friends are
sitting on the sidewalk, hands
behind their backs.

Someone pats down the
nice pants you're wearing.

Someone looks through
the car.

You can't feel
anything but numb.

The building they take
you to is familiar. A knot
forms in your throat
when you see it.

The letters and numbers
on the front.

The steps
leading up to the door.

The decades-old
wooden bench inside.

The solid black
gate you're led
through.

The desk you're
led to,

the person sitting
in your father's seat.

*Isn't that one of
Sergeant Miranda's girls?*
someone whispers.

You're too tired,
too foggy

to correct them.

To tell them you're
Sergeant Miranda's
only girl, now.

You're placed in a cell
of your own, away

from all your new friends.

Your head is throbbing.

Your eyes fall closed to
block out the light, until
you drift off.

◊

You wake to hushed tones
outside your cell.

A familiar voice asks
if this can stay quiet.

You can't hear the
answer, but the cell
clinks open and Papi
walks in.

> He looks older
> and more tired
> than you've ever
> seen him.

He won't look you
in the eye. You leave
through the back door

with both of your heads down.

You keep waiting
for him to say something.

> In the precinct
> parking lot.

> In the car on
> the way home.

> In the quiet
> of the house.

No
Good night, Peanut,
as he shuts his
bedroom door.

You keep hoping that
he'll scream or punish
you or start a fight.

But instead

you're left with a sick
feeling in your stomach and
the dead silence of your room.

Papi has never asked
for help

in his life.

Not when he could barely
afford to keep you and
Mami and Mel in an
apartment.

Not when he made
a habit of drowning
his sorrows.

Not when he had to carry
Mami out of the
hospital

without Mel.

But the next morning
you wake up in your
bed—
        throbbing head and
dry mouth and
turning stomach and all.

        Not in a cell.

        Not on your way
        to see a judge.

In your room, with
the morning sun

shining
on your mistakes.

Papi owes someone
a favor now,

        and the thought makes
        your rolling insides
        tumble a little
        more.

Mami doesn't see you
when she looks at you.

She makes breakfast as
though you're not there, slides
a plate toward you

without a word.

Later, you find her in your room:
folding your clothes and
packing them into a
suitcase.

Something in you freezes

and shatters

as you watch her pack
your life away.

Your voice is raw,
the sound ripped out of you—
            Mami?

She slams the suitcase
shut.

            We can't—
            I *can't lose you, too,*
            she says.

When she finally turns
her eyes on you,
you're not sure

what she sees.

◊

We're going to get you help,
they'd said, while Papi
made plans and Mami
packed your bags.

There's an outfit waiting
for you, like it's your
first day of school.

The rehab center is 90 minutes
away from home, through
towns and trees and
hidden roads.

This is where you live now:

> A house away from curious
> eyes.

> A sign that doesn't give
> away what's inside.

> A place with nothing to do

> but heal.

There's a wound you
keep picking at, keep

opening with thoughts
you try to avoid.

It starts to itch.

You try to remember
the last time you spent

a night
away from home.

Your new room is not
your own. You've never
shared a room
with a stranger before.

You wonder if your
roommate

can feel the sweat on your
palm as she shakes your
hand.

　　　She's not your friend,
you remind yourself.

You're on your own here.

◊

Your new room has rules:

> - Beds must have hospital
>   corners.

> - Floors must be swept
>   and mopped daily.

> - Closets must be sorted:
>   jackets, sweaters, shirts,
>   then pants.

> - All clothes must be hung
>   in the same direction.

> - All shoes must be lined
>   up under the bed with toes
>   peeking out.

You ready your new
room and ignore

the way your hands
shake.

At home, you laid
in bed and watched

lights from passing
cars dance across your
ceiling as you drifted
off.

Here,
your room is dark and
there are no lights or
shadows

to guide you to sleep.

You want to sleep
late the next morning, but

that's not allowed.

Your roommate shakes your
shoulder and warns you
of the trouble you'll be in

if you try.

Breakfast is at 8:30.

You grab a bagel and sit
alone. And you wonder

if you look sick.

If anyone can tell
why you're here. Like you
can see fading bruises on
your roommate's arms.

They all sit together
          and talk
          and laugh

like they don't know
where they are.

Like somehow
they've forgotten.

You wonder if you'll
forget after
a while.

You have another
therapist now.

He's old and
white and
nothing like Tiana.

Part of you wishes he'd
stop talking, as if he
could unravel you

after all this time.

But you sit back and
nod at the right
moments.

As long as he's
talking,

you don't have to.

Group therapy is
easier to ignore.

Easier
to fade into
the background

and listen to other
people talk.

So many of them
sound like you.

> It started at a party—

> A friend told me
> to try it—

> It happened so fast—

> It's so hard to go
> without it.

But you're not like
these people.

You're not sick.

You're not dependent.

You don't belong
here.

They call it
alternative therapy.

You roll your eyes.

It's arts and crafts.

It's band practice.

It's writing a sad
poem in your diary.

It's sitting in front
of a canvas with
a brush.

It's pretending to make
something worthwhile.

You wonder how
long you can

get away with watching
everyone else waste
their time.

You'd rather run
outside, but

a treadmill will do.

You lose yourself
in the movement—

> your sneakers hitting
> the belt.

> The numbers on the
> deck climbing higher
> the more you run.

> The way you can
> feel your pulse in
> your fingertips.

The sweat cooling
on the back of your shirt.

No one asks you
questions

or expects you
to be friendly.

No one tells you to
explain yourself.

To recount your
mistakes.

You used to live for
moments like

these, lapping
your neighborhood

on early mornings
with Mel.

But it's not the same.

Not here.

Not by yourself.

Dinner is the first time
you've ever felt this

alone

in a room full of people.

You push bland
pasta around your
plate

and long for Mami's
pollo guisado,

for Papi's *pernil*.

At lights out,

you strain to listen for
the lull of *something*, of
music from passing
cars.

Or the refrigerator humming
downstairs.

Or Papi sneaking
to watch TV when he
can't sleep.

Instead

you're stuck with

your roommate's
whisper-soft snores,

and the quiet threatens
to consume you.

Day 2

Wake Up.
Breakfast.
Group therapy.
Lunch.
Alt. therapy.
Fitness.
Dinner.
Free time.
Lights out.

There are looks when
they think you can't see—

      wondering why you
      won't speak.

      Guessing at an
      illness you swear
      you don't have.

They make you try
journaling. And you

write out the lyrics
to a song you knew

in another lifetime.

Day 3

Wake Up.
Breakfast.
Therapy.
Lunch.
Alt. therapy.
Fitness.
Dinner.
Free time.
Lights out.

Your new therapist wants
to *get to know you.*

Things that were important
before

seem like nothing now—

> things like how old
> you are,

> how school's going,

> what you want to do
> after graduation.

You wonder, later, what
things make up
who you are—

and you're not sure anymore.

◖

Day 4

Wake Up.
Breakfast.
Group therapy.
Lunch.
Alt. therapy.
Fitness.
Dinner.
Free time.
Lights out.

There's some free
time in the evening, just
before lights out.

Most people are
inside, hunched over books
or huddled together,
talking.

You're outside with a
cigarette you bummed
off of a janitor.

It's hot out—
sticky August air—

and you can feel your
hair inflating with
the heat.

Mami visits on Day 5.

She hugs you, touches
your face and hair as if
to make sure you're
really here.

You nestle your face into
her neck.

> The smell of her perfume
> makes something
> tighten in your chest.
>
> Makes your throat and
> eyes burn with feelings
> you didn't know you had.

He's working,
she tells you when
she sits down.

You haven't asked about
Papi, but you guess
you didn't need to.

He'll come when he can.

She holds your hand when
she says it but

won't look you in the eye.

Your stomach churns
when you think about Papi.

You have to pause from
fixing your bed to hold
your middle

and keep yourself grounded.

You knew—
no matter how he
denied it—

you were his favorite.

His tough girl, the one
he never worried about.

Not soft like Mel,
not in need of
constant comfort.

You were his favorite, then
his only girl.

And you ruined it.

Maybe he should have worried.

Tiana's there
just a few days later.

You never thought you'd
be relieved to see her, but

something about her box
braids tied into a bun
on top of her head

comforts you.

You're ready for her
to ask what happened on
your birthday. To ask
how you ended up here.

You're already making
up the lies. They're on
your tongue,

ready to launch.

But instead she says,
Your hair looks so good!
Asks what you've done
to it.

And your shoulders sag.

◆

This place sucks,
you think on Day 13.

The food tastes like
cardboard made in 1943.

Your phone is locked
away, except for one
hour twice a week.

The boredom is
a fog that settles deeper
with every breath.

And you don't belong here.

Was this place
meant to make you
want to *stop* drinking?

There's so much
time to think,

too many chances
to think about
all the mistakes
you've made.

Too many attempts
to fix things that can
never be unbroken.

Now more than ever
your hands itch for
a glass.

Now,
more than ever,
you long for that

hazy feeling of
indifference.

It hits you one
afternoon. Letting your
mind wander during
group therapy.
The drinking was never
the problem.

The weed was never
the problem.

The problem
was what came before.

The shame.

The guilt.

The newfound
loneliness.

The feeling of
being lost.

The need for something
to make it go away.

In your mind, the
words are screamed.

But in the room,
you're silent.

That night,
you dream about Mel.

She's sitting across from
you, in the same seat
Mami sat in when
she visited.

I like this dress,
she says, and shows you
a picture on her phone.

But I wish it was red.

She shouldn't be here.

Your hands grip the
table until your knuckles
turn white.

She can't
see you here. Can't
see how badly you've
messed up.

She's nervous—
Maybe next year,
we can go back?

Stay in San Juan?

Swim in the glowing
waters of Vieques?

She looks at you
like her whole
life hinges on your
answer. You can't—

Of course,
you tell her.

She smiles, but when
you reach for her,

she's gone.

In your waking moments,
you try to avoid
thinking about Mel.

Try to avoid going
down that rabbit hole.

Avoid the sour feelings
that storm, that rage
with thoughts of her.

But here, in quiet
moments

(so, so many
quiet moments),

you wonder what
she would do.

The first time you talk
to Tiana—*really*
talk to her—

it's almost by accident.

She asks if you miss
your friends, and you're
already reaching,

in your mind, for
a good lie.

Or a funny one, maybe.

But instead, what comes
out is:
                I don't have friends.

She stops for a second—

          Oh?

You don't even realize
it's true until
it's past your lips.

But it is true.

> You have people
> you know.

> People who fill
> your cup.

> Who dare you to
> do another shot.

> Who pass the joint
> to you.

> And laugh when you
> cough or throw
> up in a bush.

> Who hang you
> out to dry when
> you get pulled over
> by a cop, but—

>> *My best friend is dead,*
>> you tell her.

She nods.

>> *Tell me about that.*

And you do.

You call Mami
one afternoon.

She talks about painting
the kitchen, about
your aunt asking
how you're doing.

She says Papi is busy.
(He's always busy.)

Through the window, you
see a woman tending
to the plants outside.

It strikes you that she
may be the only other
brown-skinned person here.

You watch her gloved
hands working the
soil—

        I'm sorry, Mami,
        you say suddenly.

Mami stops talking.

        For what, baby?

You've lost track of
the things you're sorry for.

You're by the side of
the building, smoking
a cigarette

the next time you see
the woman in the garden.

She grunts every time
she bends to work the
earth, rubs at her
back when she stands.

You stomp out your
cigarette. Wipe the
sweat off your
palms. Walk over and
ask if you can help.

She looks you
over. Hesitates.

You can pull the weeds.

So you pull the weeds.

Her name is Luz.

She pulls an extra
pair of gloves out
of her pocket.

Shows you which
ones are weeds.

Shows you how to
loosen the soil around
the roots.

How to pick out the
thickest root.

To pull until there's
nothing left, make sure
there are no remains.

When you're done,
there's an ache in
your shoulders that
grounds you.

The breath you
sigh out

leaves you feeling lighter.

He blames himself,
Mami tells you, the
next time you see her.

She brought *pastelillos*.

You take another bite
and keep your eyes
down when you nod.

You don't blame Papi
for not wanting to see you.

But you still wish
he were here to say so.

That he'd give you a
chance to tell him
it's not his fault.

But he won't even call.

Outside in the
garden, Luz is showing
you how to prune.

>*You have to cut away*
>*the dead parts to*
>*help it grow,*

>she says, and hands
>you the shears.

You're about to press
the blade to a stem

when you hear a car
rolling over the
gravel driveway.

But it's not Papi
like you'd hoped.

And that growing pit
in your stomach
widens.

Deepens.

You take a breath.

And trim the stem.

Isn't this
what you wanted?

All those times you
dreamed of leaving
home.

Of being independent,
of getting away.

Of living a life that
was just yours, that you
didn't share with Mel.

That Mami didn't
watch with worried
eyes.

That you could live
outside of Papi's
shadow.

> But maybe they weren't
> the problem.
>
> Maybe it's in you,
> under your skin.
>
> Following and driving
> every mistake.

The next time
in the garden,

Luz hands you a
pot with a flowering
plant.

Time to plant the pansies,
she says.

She takes you through
the steps.

Mix the compost in.

Dig the hole.

Empty the pot,
loosen the roots
with your hand.

The soil sticks to
your glove as you
lower the plant
into the ground.

You cover the roots
and sit back.

Your throat burns.

Your eyes water,
and spill over when
you blink.

Soon your breath
shudders with
heaving sobs.

Your tears fall onto
freshly tilled soil.

When was the last time
you did good?

Created?

Made something more
beautiful

instead of destroying it?

I knew.

Tiana waits for you
to keep going.

It's the first time
you've said it out loud.

You tell yourself you're
only talking because you're
bored, but you keep
going.

You knew that Mel was not okay.

You knew one day she might
take it
        too
              far.

You knew something was
wrong

and you did nothing.

You breathe the words
into the world,

and the only thing that
changes

is you.

You tell Tiana
about the first time you
knew something was wrong.

Twelve years old,
walking into the
bedroom you shared
with Mel.

The blank stare in Mel's
red-rimmed eyes where
they were trained on
her feet.

      I'm tired,
      she'd said.

You'd told her to nap,
didn't know yet what
she'd really meant:

      Tired of existing
      in a life she
      didn't want.

      A life she would
      never learn
      to want.

A life you could
have helped,

but didn't.

You tell yourself
you're okay.

You always tell
yourself that you're
okay.

But if you were,

maybe Mel would still
be here.

But instead
your parents were
burdened

with two messed-up girls.

It's no wonder Papi
won't talk to you.

Tiana pauses.
Sighs.

Hesitates, for
the first time

since you've known her.

> *Do you think he blames you?*
> she asks.

You shrug.
He should.

She nods, stops
again, searches
for the right words.

> *You need to talk to him.*

For the first
time, you agree.

Papi visits on a Tuesday,

six weeks after
you arrived here.

The school year is about
to start, and you're not
there.

You and Luz have
started planting bulbs. She
says they'll flower in
the spring.

> They need some time
> in the cold
> before they can bloom.

Papi brings a pack
of playing cards.

He cuts the deck, gives
you your hand.

Your hands
shake as the cards
move across the table.

> *You're not the only one,*
> he says after
> a while.

You hold your cards
without making a move.

> You knew about Papi,
> about his drinking.

You were there
the night he fired
his gun through his
bedroom wall.

The patch
of plaster is still there.

But he tells you
about his brothers,
John and Miguel
and Ray,
all with their
own addictions.

Through needles,
through smoke,
through powder
or bottles.

They always found
what they were
looking for.

About your
bipolar cousin.

You never got to
meet her before
it was too late.

Your aunt's
psychosis.

The way she struggled
between the things she
saw and heard

and what
she knew to be true.

Your grandfather's
trauma.

Papi growing up
with a father who
never quite came home.

Your sister's—

Mel was still
alive when you found
her, hand reaching
out to you—

The card game
is over.

Instead the table is
laid out with

a family tree
full of illness.

> *You and Mel are*
> *sick because of me,*
> Papi tells you.

He reaches for you,
but stops short.

> *Tienes la misma sangre—*

> *You have the same*
> *blood.*

◖

A week later
you haven't stopped

thinking about what
Papi said.

>   *The family never
>   talked about it.*

For a second
you saw in Papi

the same weight
you've been carrying
for seven months.

>   *Maybe we should have.*

You think about Mel,
fighting a beast
that had been with her
since birth.

A beast that may be
in you, too.

There's a new boy
here, if you can
call him that.

He must be a boy
if he's here, but

calling him that feels
wrong, somehow.

Like the *boy* is buried
beneath his shaved
head and pale, blotchy

skin, half-covered
in tattoos.

Tattoos that are
starting to fade, ones
with thick black
lines.

And sharp edges that
peek out from under
the collar of his shirt.

He watches you,
sometimes—

you see him from
the corner of your
eye. Glaring at you

from under thin, wispy
eyebrows.

A stare that raises
the hair on the back

of your neck

and makes your
stomach turn sour.

You avoid him as
much as you can.

Luz is making you
haul evergreen
saplings

to the other
side of the yard.

He's there, behind
the building, smoking
and watching.

Luz's hand squeezes
your arm, hurries
you along.

> *Stay away from him*,
> she warns, voice
> low.

She doesn't know
him, but—

> *I've seen faces*
> *like that before.*

She rubs at a
scar on the side
of her throat,

and won't say
another word.

You feel his eyes
on you, even
when he's not
there.

From across the
room at breakfast.

As you tune out
in group therapy.

He's outside the
fitness room when
you step off the
treadmill.

Always looking,
but you're not sure

what for.

You haven't quite
spilled your story
to your new therapist.

But it's getting easier.

On your way out of
his office, you're
thinking about your
next steps.

Suddenly
someone rams into
your shoulder—

> *Watch where you're*
> *going, spic.*

He's no boy.

You can see that now.

You're backed against
a wall while he
inches closer—

Was he always
this tall?

Why don't you
go back where
you came from?

You try to keep
your eyes on his
hands, get ready
to run—

Your therapist's door
squeaks open and he
steps into the hall—

Elena? Is there
a problem?

The boy backs
away.

No problem here.

He walks away, and
your legs bend and
fall beneath you.

Your hands are still
shaking when you
get back to your room.

You take stock of
the world around
you, ground yourself.

Look in the mirror.

> You left your hair
> straightener at home,
>
> and your curls are
> back in full force.
>
> Like a dark brown halo
> framing your face.

Your skin has
darkened after hours
spent in the
garden with Luz.

◆

Spic is not a new
word

but you never thought
you'd hear it aimed
at you.

Mami always explained
it to you

as someone ignorant,
uneducated,

who'd never make it
off the island.

As if that made it
okay to use the
word as a weapon.

> Was this how Mel
> felt? Always visible,
> always exposed?

Your skin has never
made you feel

unsafe

until now.

It's no surprise
that you think of Mel.

You imagine her
taking on that
boy, defending you
at all costs.

It makes you smile.

Mel never tried to
hide the way you did.

> You laugh,
> bitterly.

Hiding.

As if you could ever

really hide.

As if people
like *him*

could ever look
at you

and not see who
you really are.

You remember Mel,

standing behind you
in the bathroom mirror.

Watching you straighten
your hair, use makeup

just a shade too light.

>*Who do you think
>you're fooling?*

Your fingertips go
numb.

You're not fooling
anyone.

You never have,

you never will.

There is nowhere left

for you to hide.

My name is Elena.

It's the first
time you've ever
spoken

in group therapy.

For a moment
the eyes on you tie
your tongue and make
you regret

opening your mouth.

But you square your
shoulders and press on.

Your name is Elena.

You're sick.

And that's okay.

You let yourself
have names.

Let yourself call
your roommate Jess.

> Sit with her at
> breakfast and talk
> about her dog.

> He's a golden lab
> named Steve, and she
> can't wait to get back
> home to him.

You let yourself call
your therapist by his
name—Gary—

> and you don't know
> much about him, but.

> You let him know you.

> You tell him about Mel.

The boy with the
tattoos is called
Ryan.

You don't want
to know him, but

putting a name to
the fear helps you
face it.

There are others—

names and
faces and
stories—

you let yourself
know them.

Let yourself
plant roots.

Let them be
a part of you

getting better.

Weeks pass.

Time seems to move
differently here.

      Slower, almost,

in seconds and
minutes, in words
and growing pains.

And yet, before
you know it,

Gary says
you're going home.

      How do you
      feel about that?
      he asks. Waits
      for your reply.

And, well.

How *do* you feel
about that?

Gary and Tiana have
taught you to be
present, in what you
feel. To own it.

You take stock.

There's some
excitement—

it bubbles up and
threatens to burst.

> The thought of
> being home.

> Sleeping in
> your own bed.

> Having Mami and
> Papi near again.

> The chance to rebuild.

Some sadness,
too.

Bittersweet.

As you look out
over the garden
you built with Luz.

You created
life here—

things you don't
want to leave
behind.

Reminders

that you can
do something good.

Can make things

grow.

But mostly

there's fear.

> Going home means
> going back to
> where this started.

Back to the life
where you lost

your best friend.

> Without drinks.
> Without your friends.
> Without school

to pull you
away from the
feelings.

No choice but
to live in it.

You breathe—

Ground yourself
in this moment.

Look at the feeling.

Know it.

Let it pass.

Remind yourself that
you don't have to
do it alone.

        Not like Mel did.

Can you
forgive yourself?
Someday?

Tiana is with you
in the garden.

You're going home
soon.

She'll be with you,
she says,

to help you make
sense of what
comes after.

You don't know
what forgiveness

looks like.

Not yet.

But you'd like
to find out.

You're packing your
things when you
hear the news.

Jackets, sweaters,
shirts, then pants.

All folded, neat
and square, into
your suitcase.

You've learned to
find peace in
order.

In taking
control of your
world.

Some people are
in the TV room.

The news is on.

Something heavy like
lead drops

into your stomach.

The hurricane rips
through Puerto Rico

like blades through
water.

      Twisting everything
      in its wake.

Cars overturned.

Homes torn down
to their beams.

Trees downed, taking
power lines with them.

Roads drowned in
brown, still water.

◊

You walked those
roads with Mel once,

years ago.

Leaned against
those trees, rocked

back and forth to
shake coconuts loose
from their tops.

    But

    you don't see
    roads or trees.

    Don't see buildings
    or power lines
    or cars.

You see Marianella.

The parts of her she
left on the island.

The only parts of her
she loved.

Maybe the only home
she ever felt safe in—

    gone.

Today was supposed
to be better.

Today you're going home.

Your bags are packed.

> Your phone is
> full of
> numbers from all
> your new friends.

Luz brings you
a Christmas rose
in an orange pot.

But you move in
a daze.

> Images of Puerto
> Rico shuffle
> through your mind.

How many dead—

> how many still
> in the dark?

Mami and Papi
still have family

on the island.

> You want to ask but
> you don't want
> to know.

> > *Nothing yet*,
> > Mami says.

She dials her sister's
number for the
hundredth time.

Papi's hand shakes
as he calls his father.

No answer.

> No answers.

You're just
starting to unpack.

Your hands ache
to do something—

    to build,

    to create.

To save the
memories of
your sister

left across the water.

    We have to go,

    you tell Mami and
    Papi.

    Suitcase in hand.

You have to.

Tiana makes sure
you understand
before you go.

       It won't
       bring Mel back.

You know this.

       It won't
       cure you.

You know this
too.

But you still
have guilt.

Have fear.

Have shame.

       You're going to
       do something

       with it.

Getting a flight
to Puerto Rico

      isn't easy.
      Or fast.

But you and Mami
and Papi
make it.

      The last time you
      set foot on this
      island, Mel

      stood beside you.

Trees and
stalled cars and
pieces of homes

block the road.

You get out
of the truck,

and you walk.

Mami and Papi's
families live

in the mountains.

You're caked in
grime and
sweat and
mud

when you arrive.
But there it is.

Your blood rushes
to your head
at the sight.
Your feet rooted
to the ground.

The last time Mel
was here, she found

blue tiles in the grass,

remnants

of a home that once was.
The tiles are gone.

So are the horses.

There are craters
in the soil

    where coffee bushes
    have been ripped
    from the ground.

Someone emerges
from the shambles

of what was
once a house:

Mami's sister.

Weary.

Alive.
Papi's father is gone.

Papi falls to his
knees when he hears
the news.

> He does it again
> when he sees the
> unmarked plot where
> his father is buried.

They say it
happened fast.
That he didn't
suffer.

> That they couldn't
> call Papi to tell him—
> no power, no phone.

Papi's sitting alone,
covered in dirt,
head in hands
when you find him.

Papi, I'm so—

> *Not now, Peanut.*

You nod.

You'll be here
waiting.
You get to work.

Mami helps her
sister make sense
of the wreckage—

helps her find
more help where
she can.

> Papi isn't ready
> to talk—

> he does what he can
> to rebuild home.

> Finds scraps of
> supplies where he
> can.

> Works until his hands
> crack and bleed.

>> He's not okay.
>> But he will be.

You—

You keep digging.

For purpose.
For new life.

> For the memories
> of Marianella
> that linger in
> the earth here.

You find coffee
beans

and get to work.

> Till the soil.

> Dig the hole.

> Plant the seeds.

Keep digging
for the hope

that lies beneath.

WANT TO KEEP READING?

If you liked this book, check out another book

from West 44 Books:

EVERY LITTLE BAD IDEA
BY CAITIE MCKAY

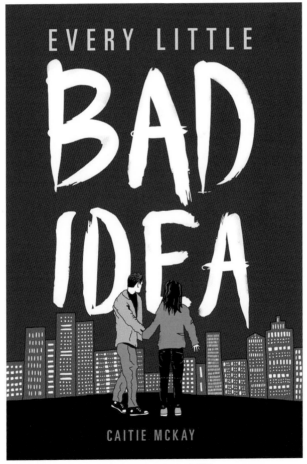

ISBN: 9781538382653

NO CHOICE

but to try harder.

No choice

but to fly higher.

You see,
Grandmom had Mom
when she was only 18.

You see,
Mom only made it
to junior year
before she had me.

You see,
Mom says,
*The women in this
family have a
        w e a k n e s s
for bad boys.*

But not me.

No.

That could
never be.

ABOUT THE AUTHOR

M. Azmitia is a government employee by day and a poet/cat lady by night in New York City. She holds a degree in English and creative writing. Azmitia writes about Latinidad and mental health in the hopes of starting a conversation about the stigma of mental illness in communities of color.

Check out more books at:
www.west44books.com

An imprint of Enslow Publishing

WEST **44** BOOKS™